James Ambrose Story

Carmina silvulae

Poems Original and Translated

James Ambrose Story

Carmina silvulae
Poems Original and Translated

ISBN/EAN: 9783337206963

Printed in Europe, USA, Canada, Australia, Japan

Cover: Foto ©Andreas Hilbeck / pixelio.de

More available books at **www.hansebooks.com**

CARMINA SILVULAE

POEMS

ORIGINAL AND TRANSLATED

BY

JAMES AMBROSE STORY, B.A.

> "Of every flower you sip,
> Little bee, with honied lip!"
> "Yes," said the bee, as he poised in air,
> "Yes, but I leave the poison there."
>
> p 84.

LONDON

AUTHORS' CO-OPERATIVE PUBLISHING CO., Ltd.

20 AND 22 ST. BRIDE STREET, E.C.

1890

CONTENTS.

iv Contents.

DEDICATION.

To thee, whose lips first bade me write,
    whose smile
My earliest efforts paid ; to thee, whose
    face,
Thro' mist of time, I now but dimly trace—
Thro' mist of tears, that often spring, the
    while
On that loved countenance I sadly dwell ;
To thee, of whom it yet doth glad my
    heart
To think, that, ere from earth thou didst
    depart,
I had done something that did please
    thee well ;
To thee, dear mother, now in peace above,
This little book I fondly have address'd,
A tribute to thy faith, thy truth, thy love.
Ah ! from that happy seat where thou dost
    dwell
With him, who long before had gone to
    rest,
Look down on thine, yet toss'd on ocean's
    swell !

ODE TO FANCY.

COME, sprightly Fancy, cheerful
     wight,
     Come in gayest livery dight,
Or a sunbeam blithely sporting,
Or on frolic Zephyr floating ;
Come awhile and stay with me,
Then will I thy follower be.

Wake me ere the break of morn,
Ere the lark, on ether borne,
Hath left his little grass-made nest,
And shook the dew from off his crest ;
Long ere the early rising bee
Hath left his hive in hollow tree,
And to the fragrant heather flown,
Or to the flower-spread meadow gone.

Let us haste to see the sun,
While the morn is grey and dun,
Tip yon eastern hills with gold,
And one by one his beams unfold,

And dart them thro' the misty sky,
Till the gloom away doth fly.
Thro' the meadows then we'll go,
By breezes fanned, that round us blow,
And listen to the birds all singing,
And hear the woodman's hatchet ringing;
While as the frequent strokes resound,
Sly echo mocks with mimic sound.

See the dewdrops glistening bright
On each leaflet ! To the sight
They seem like glittering pearlets all,
While the sunbeams on them fall.
Come, we'll pluck a nosegay rare
Of all the flowers that bloom so fair,
Then afar we'll slowly wander
Where doth this little brook meander,
And watch the fishes in it sporting,
And bending flowers its kisses courting.

Thro' yon thick and shady wood,
That for countless years hath stood,
Now we'll stray, among the trees
That softly woo the passing breeze.
Beneath some gnarled old oak we'll sit,
Among whose boughs the finches flit :
And we'll think of Druids old,
Who, in these shades, the Britons told,

In the midnight dark and bleak,
When the night wind round did shriek,
'Twas the cry of spirits damned,
For disobeying their command ;—
Now doomed for aye, at midnight drear,
To howl before the storm's career,
Among the waving branches dashed,
And by those waving branches lashed.

It may be that in yonder glade
Some dreadful sacrifice was made.
Perhaps upon the altar stone
The struggling victim thither drawn
Was stretched, and in his quivering
    breast
The sacrificial blade was pressed.
Perhaps the fearful image reared,
With shrieking victims full, appeared ;
And then, while bards attuned the lyre,
The white-robed priest applied the fire ;
And soon they drowned the dreadful cry
With shouts and noisy revelry.
Eventide comes on apace,
Soon the sun will end his race.
As we gaze on western skies,
Where in rosy bed he lies,
Lo ! the clouds take strangest shapes—
Castles, dragons, giants, apes,

And we think of many a knight
Wandering thro' the land to fight
All whom he found the weak oppressing,
And all the wrongs he found redressing ;
Or we think of castles grim,
In whose dungeons deep and dim
Fair dames were held in durance hard
By cruel foe or ruthless lord.

Lo, the scene is dark around !
And the ear arrests no sound
Save the brooklet's sweet, soft fluting,
Or the owlet harshly hooting ;
Or, perchance, some little bird
Chirping at intervals is heard
From its nest within the thorn ;
Or on stilly air is borne
The muffled sound of distant bell
Ringing out day's parting knell !

Now we dream of fairies dancing,
Of elfins in the moonbeams prancing,
And fancy in the shade we see,
'Neath the leaves of some low tree,
Puck with merry twinkling eye
Peering at us passing by.
And we dream of Fay-queen Mab,
With her dainty snail-shell cab ;

Of Oberon, and of his queen,
And all their sports upon the green ;
And every floweret seems a sprite
Dancing in the pale moonlight !
   1862.

———

LEONIDAS.

EONIDAS, when shall thy name
No more the patriot soul in-
flame ?
When shall the brave three hundred die ?
When perish their proud memory ?
Their dauntless eyes beheld the foe,
Unmoved they stood in serried row,
Their swords and spears flashed in the
    light,
Their burnished helms shone glittering
    bright,
And like a lion couched they stood,
Or like a rock against the flood,
Until the clarion's dreadful sound
Awoke the echoing hills around ;
Then the warriors' war pæan rose,
Soft as the zephyr, when it blows
Over the woods at silent eve,
Sweet as the strains the swan doth give

When dying she a voice doth find—
So rose their death-strain on the wind.
And to the swelling tones they tread
Advancing, 'gainst the foemen led ;
And as their feet the nearer drew,
And as the strain more mighty grew,
Upon that countless host they rushed,
From many a heart the life-blood gushed,
In many a breast their spears were thrust,
And many a Persian kissed the dust.
Then raged the contest fierce and loud ;
Their bosoms with wild ardour glowed ;
And side by side those Spartans fought,
Their death by Persia's best blood bought.
A hundred foes for each that fell
Were plunged into the depths of hell,
And Xerxes' proudest and best mailed
Before that band of heroes quailed.
As fights a tigress for her young,
While red spears flashed and trumpet rung,
Long, long those Spartans fearless fought,
None turned his back, none safety sought.
But one by one they nobly die ;
Surrounded by their foes they lie ;
Till, when no Spartan more remained,
Their foes a dreadful victory gained.
The green grass grows upon their graves,
The olive there its branches waves ;
Their bodies mingle with the dust,

And 'neath the sod their weapons rust,
But oh ! their name shall live for ever,
The glory of their land for ever.
   1862.

TO A CHILD.

ON HER NINTH BIRTHDAY.

HOU'R'T nine years old, and on
    thy brow,
     As smooth as summer skies I
trow,
No sorrow hath its mask imprest,
No trace is found of heart's unrest.

A few years more will pass away—
A few short years how brief their stay !
And then, thy childhood with them flown,
Thy heart will many a care have known.

A few years more ! Ah ! where are they
Who in thy youth did with thee play ?
All, all are gone—like shadows pass'd—
And thou alone art left at last.

So childhood, youth and age shall fly
Like sunbeams in an April sky,
Like dreams that flit thro' childish minds,
Like leaves that float on Autumn winds !
   1862.

CHILDHOOD, YOUTH AND AGE.

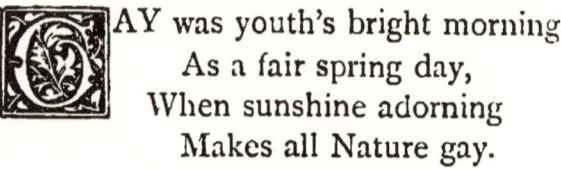AY was youth's bright morning
  As a fair spring day,
When sunshine adorning
  Makes all Nature gay.

Fled the hours by gladly
  With a laughing glee,
Ne'er my heart beat sadly,
  All was joy to me.

Summer-time came after
  With a soberer dye,
Softer was my laughter,
  Staider was my eye.

Still my days were gladness,
  All was fair to view ;
Little knew I sadness,
  Thoughts of care soon flew.

But the hours fast fled on,
  Autumn soon was nigh,
And as years now sped on,
  So did youth's dream fly.

Things now lost the colour
  Which in youth shone gay ;

So a flower—you cull her,
And she fades away.

Winter-time approaches,
Mournful is his guise ;
Slowly he encroaches,
As the Autumn dies.

Gone are childhood's fancies,
Gone is youth's glad dream,
Naught illusive glances,
Things are what they seem.

1862.

———

THE OLD YEAR'S DEATH.

NOT a sound broke on the ear,
Save the dying year's low sigh :
And as the hours passed by,
Sometimes a moan you'd hear.

And many a bright star peeping
With glistering, mournful eye
Was watching thoughtfully,
A solemn vigil keeping.

And the young moon look'd on too,
As she sailed across the sky
Among the clouds, which by
Majestically flew.

If the frost-king then was out,
    So noiselessly moved he,
    One thought not he could be
His wonted task about.

And listen ! Hark the sigh,
    That falleth on the ear !
    Is that a moan I hear ?
Alas ! the year must die !

Listen ! another sigh !
    Now is his last breath welling !
    Now is the bell his requiem telling !
Good-bye, old year, good-bye !

———

IN BONDS.

FRET not, dear soul, ah, fret not
        so ;
    The galling chain that fetters
        thee,
Shall break ere long, and set thee free.

Thou'rt like a bird, imprisoned fast,
That feels the Spring in all its veins,
And at its fetters chafes and strains ;

And longs to break them and away
Fly to its fellows in the grove ;—
In vain ; the bars it cannot move :

And almost bursts its swelling heart
With grief and anguish, thus to be
Fettered and caged, when all are free.

But do not fret, dear soul, ah, no !
Thy chains shall break, and thou shalt
    soar,
And never feel a fetter more.

———

THE POET AND THE WAVES.

Poet.

ERRY wavelets, sparkling bright,
    In the sunshine's golden light,
    Joyous dancers, laughing gay,
While your gambols ye do play,
Happy creatures, tell to me,
Why so light of heart ye be.

Waves.

Brightly beams the morning sun,
Briskly blow the breezes on,

Cheerily, yonder trees among,
Chaunt the birds their matin song ;
All are gay as gay can be ;
Wherefore, mortal, should not we ?

———

THE CUCKOO.

WELCOME! welcome! lonely bird!
　　Sweet thy voice to me,
Distant in the woodland heard,
　　Sounding mournfully !

Well I love to hear thy song
　　Floating in the air,
When, the silent woods among,
　　I listen to it there.

When a child I wandered oft
　　After thee, strange bird,
When from forth some distant croft,
　　Thy known note was heard.

Oh, I would that I, like thee,
　　Solitary thing,
To the lonely woods might flee
　　On unfettered wing !

In the forest, freely roaming,
  After thee I'd stray,
With the joyous Spring-time coming,
  With autumn going away.
1862.

————

NATURE'S MUSIC.

RIPPLING of waters,
    Singing of birds,
  Whispering of soft wind,
    Songs without words,

Nature's own voices,
    O'er land and sea,
These are the melodies
    Sweetest to me.

Man hath no music
    Worthy to please,
But what he deftly
    Copies from these.

When the heart's weary,
    And needeth rest,
Nature's own voices
    Soothe it the best.

EARTHLY JOYS.

HE lovely colours of the spring,
  Soon, soon decay ;
The birds, that then so sweetly
    sing,
Soon fly away.

The rose, that now so fairly blooms,
  Blooms but to-day ;
The flowers that have sweetest perfumes,
  Make shortest stay.

Earth's greatest joys, soonest depart :
  Love naught too well ;
Lest, when 'tis gone, a bleeding heart
  Thine anguish tell.

———

TO THE CHRISTIAN.

TRANGER in this world of sin,
  Christian, strive the prize to win,
  Onward, upward, ever press,
Ever in thy work progress,
Till thou reach that happy home
Whence thy feet shall never roam.

Do not linger on the way,
Do not for a moment stay,
Let not earthly joys deceive thee,
Let not man's derision grieve thee,
Keep the straight, the narrow road,
Onward to thy bright abode.

Snares on every side shall meet thee,
Satan's wiles shall ever greet thee,
Be thou brave, the victory's thine,
Doubt not, shrink not, ne'er repine,
Only let thy Faith be bright,
Thou shalt conquer in the fight.

Onward, Christian, onward hie,
Behold yon mansion in the sky;
Noble is thy aim and pure,
Only to the end endure,
Soon the contest shall be past,
Thou shalt reach thy home at last.

Angel eyes are watching o'er thee,
Glorious are the joys before thee;
There a crown awaits thy brow,
Untold pleasures thou shalt know.
Onward, Christian, onward hie,
On to Immortality !

"LORD, I FOLLOW THEE.

LORD, I come ; now naught shall
        stay me,
    Friends, nor home, tho' dear
        they be ;
Dearer far the bond that draws me :
    Lord, I follow Thee.

Not a moment will I linger ;
    But from all to Thee I flee ;
Earthly joys, away ! I leave ye !
    Lord, I follow Thee.

Be it joy, or be it sorrow,
    Be it care, 'tis naught to me ;
Lord, I come, where'er Thou leadest ;
    Lord, I follow Thee.

Onward now, nor, backward turning,
    Shall my soul regretful be,
Onward, where the Red-Cross leadeth,
    Lord, I follow Thee.
1865.

———

"LORD, REMEMBER ME."

WHILE upon life's road I travel,
    Lest I gay and thoughtless be,
    Trifling on my heavenward
        journey,
    Lord, remember me !

When fair scenes, my eyes alluring,
  Tempt me to depart from Thee,
And in danger's path I wander,
    Lord, remember me !

When the wiles, my soul enticing,
  Of the foe spread round I see,
Lest those wiles to sin should lead me,
    Lord, remember me !

And oh ! should my soul, unthinking,
  Of my Friend forgetful be,
And, in sin, should I remember,
    Lord, remember me !

When the storm around me gathers,
  And in woe I look to Thee,
Lest I perish in the tempest,
    Lord, remember me !

When sharp pangs upon me gather,
  When all earthly comforts flee,
And with pain this form is heaving,
    Lord, remember me !

And, at length, in life's last moments,
  When death's dreary stream I see,
And the dark cold valley's shadows,
    Lord, remember me !

1865.

THE VESPER HYMN.

OMPANIONS, now the day is o'er·
The sun now lights another shore,
The even-tide hath come once
more ;—
Come sing our Vesper Hymn.

The stars light up the darker sky ;
The moon sails on in majesty ;—
They sing their Maker's praise on high,
In strains unheard by us.

Morning and noon and eve and night,
All tell their great Creator's might ;
Creation sings, in depth and height,
His awful majesty.

The earth is Thine, O Lord ; the sun
At Thy behest his course doth run ;
By mighty storms Thy will is done ;
For thou dost rule o'er all.

Our feeble, trembling tongues would fain
Attempt Thy praise in fitting strain ;
But, Lord, we do attempt in vain
To sing Thy worthy praise.

But yet our songs, though weak they be,
Are swelled by notes from land and sea ;
And saints and angels, nearer Thee,
Join in our Vesper Hymn.

THE CREATOR.

ORD of the Universe, how vast
And wondrous is Thy mighty power!
Thou rul'st the raging of the blast,
And guid'st the dew-drop to the flower.

In the far depths of distant time,
Thy stern command dark Chaos heard ;
And instant, at the word sublime,
The huge, dark mass with life was stirred.

The incumbent darkness, hanging o'er
The space immense with massy weight,
Confessed the great Creator's power,
And burst into a glorious light.

Sun, moon, and stars obey Thy will,
And, led by Thee, their courses run ;
Thou bid'st the fiercest storm be still ;
By great and small Thy will is done.

And shall a feeble worm of earth
Dare challenge such celestial might ?
Shall puny man, of paltry birth,
Against the great Creator fight ?

Nay, rather, let his soul adore,
And let his tongue burst forth to praise
Such goodness, joined to such dread
    power,
Such majesty, unto such grace.
  1865.

THE MARTYR.

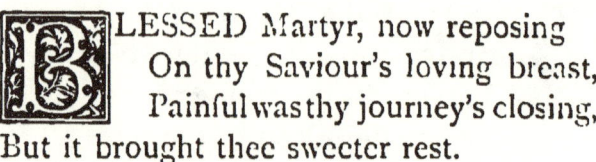LESSED Martyr, now reposing
 On thy Saviour's loving breast,
 Painful was thy journey's closing,
But it brought thee sweeter rest.

Soldier of the cross victorious,
Noble champion of the right,
Bright thy triumph was and glorious,—
Well thou won'st the bitter fight.

And with voices sweetly sounding
Angels sang the victor strain ;
While the heavenly halls resounding
Echoed back the glad refrain.

Then, while palms were strewn around
  thee,
All along the golden way
Christ Himself as victor crowned thee,
And put on thy white array.

Blessed martyr, now reposing
On thy Saviour's loving breast,
Painful was thy journey's closing,
But it brought thee sweeter rest.

 1865.

THE NIGHT IS COMING.

SINNER, flee ; the night is coming,
　　And the storm is gathering
　　　round ;
Lo ! within the distance looming,
List the thunder's louder sound ;
Threatening clouds are gathering fast,
Howleth wild the furious blast.

See, the vessel still is waiting,
That shall bear thee o'er the flood ;
Quickly hasten, nor debating,
Trifle in that doubting mood ;
Danger cannot reach thee there,
It shall thee in safety bear.

Oh ! delay not till the morrow,
For the morrow ne'er may come ;
Linger still, and thou in sorrow
May'st bewail a sinner's doom !
Hasten now, nor stay nor pause ;
Quickly nigh the moment draws.

Jesus 'tis the Vessel guideth ;
What can hurt, when He is nigh ?
Safe across the waste it rideth,
Wind and wave still neath His eye ;
Sinner, come, no moment stay ;
Hell may punish each delay.

AD ANGELUM CUSTODEM.

NGEL of God, whose presence
  bright
   Ever accompanies me,
Thy form, though clothed in heavenly light,
 My dim eyes cannot see.

And yet, at night, thy loving face
 Sometimes upon me beams ;
And then, at morn, I strive to trace,
 What I have seen in dreams.

We do not see such smiles as thine
 On earthly faces glow !
From Heaven alone such light can shine,
 Unseen on earth below.

Perchance, when time with me is o'er,—
 Ah God, so may it be !—
My opened eyes for evermore
 That blissful smile shall see !

AD MARIAM.

H, Virgin Mother ! thy loving face
  Beameth upon thy child
   Down from thy niche in the
 chapel wall
With holy smile and mild.

Gazing on thy dear countenance,
  My soul transported seems
To see thy face in heaven above
  Shine in life's glowing streams.

Ah ! mother dear, my weary heart
  Ever to thee doth flee,
When suffering from earth's bitter pain,
  Or man's inconstancy.

How darksome were life's pilgrimage
  Without thy tender love
The drooping heart, desponding soul,
  To raise to heaven above !

Mother, I make this one request,—
  Whate'er my lot may be,
Grant, when life's troubled course is o'er,
  My place may be with thee.

THE HOLY FAMILY.

C HILD of the Virgin, Thou
  Mightiest of helpers art,
  When trouble presses on the
    mind,
  Or sorrow fills the heart.

To Thee I e'er will flee
    For ease in every pain,
As wearied hind finds hidden springs,
    And seeks those springs again.

Mary, dear mother, thou
    Of mothers art the best ;
No child of earth e'er came to thee,
    But with thee he found rest.

Oft have I sought thine aid,—
    Oft sought it tearfully ;
But never have I sighed unheard,
    Never in vain to thee.

Blest Joseph, loving saint,
    To thee what shall I say ?
As now, so ever, blessed saint,
    Support me on my way.

Jesus, Lord of sweet love,
    Mary, our mother dear,
And Joseph, universal sire,
    Ever your suppliants hear !

———

SPRING-TIDE.

HE first bright day of Spring-tide,
Sunny, and warm, and glad,
Light'ning the load of sorrow,
Cheering the heart that's sad !

The first sweet bird of Spring-tide,
Singing upon the spray,
Filling the soul with its music,
Chasing the gloom away !

The first fair flower of Spring-tide,
Blooming there all alone,
Bright'ning the earth with its smiling,
Telling that winter is gone !

Dawn of the Spring-tide eternal,
Birds whose songs never cease,
Flowers breathing fragrance for ever,
Come with your joy and your peace !

———

MUSINGS.

IND, it is infinite,
Speech hath its bounds ;
Hearts have their motions
Where lips have no sounds.

Thoughts there are higher
  Than ears ever heard ;
Feelings profounder
  Than ever found word :

Greater imaginings,
  Sentiments truer ;
Nobler sympathies,
  Longings more pure ;

Thoughts that are God-like,
  Higher than earth ;
Feelings beseeming
  Heavenly birth.

———

DESTRUCTION OF THE FIRST-BORN.

TWAS night, silent night, in the
    land of the Nile,
    And the moon lit the river's
broad breast with her smile ;
Over mountain and valley and city she
  beamed,
On pyramid, temple, and palace she
  gleamed.

Over all the Egyptians reigned sleep still
    as death,—
The silence unbroke e'en by zephyr's soft
    breath;
Not a breeze moved the leaves of the tall
    stately palm;
All, all was quite motionless, silent, and
    calm.

And thro' the dim twilight a spirit flew by;
'Twas the Angel of Death, with his sword
    raised on high.
He flashed like a meteor thro' the air on
    his way,
And he entered the homes, where the
    sleeping ones lay.

And the sleepers sleep on till the morning
    is nigh;
And then—Oh, the wail that ascends to
    the sky!
In each home in the land, stiff and cold
    on his bed,
The first-born lies motionless, speechless,
    and dead.

Thro' the land there was wailing, and
    weeping, and woe;

For from east unto west, mid the high and
    the low,
There was not a home that had felt not
    the stroke,—
Not a house but to sorrow and mourning
    awoke.

———

THE GREAT BOOK.

HERE is a ponderous volume,
    Where all our words are writ;
Its leaves are seen in Heaven,
    And in Hell's gloomy pit.

Some gleam in glory brighter
    Than sun hath ever shone;
Some glare in darkness blacker
    Than Hell hath ever known.

The good man's word of kindness,
    The bad man's words of hate,
The bitter curse, the blessing,
    The words of small and great,

There full 'twixt Hell and Heaven
    They stand, or black, or bright;

Nor fiend, nor happy angel,
　But doth behold the sight.

And no good word is ever
　Upon that wide page writ,
But the Almighty's countenance
　With a sweet smile is lit.

That smile all Heaven illumines
　With its effulgence bright ;
The face of every angel
　Reflects that smile of light.

But oh, when words of evil
　Are written on that leaf,
In Hell, the fiendish laughter
　Tells that in Heaven is grief.

Each angel's face is shrouded
　To hide the dreadful sight ;
The Almighty's face is clouded,
　And none behold its light.

Each word, not only from the lips,
　But from the heart as well,
Gladdens God's happy angels,
　Or gladdens fiends in Hell.

Each word! each thought ! Oh! may
    there be
Nor word, nor thought of thine,
But, writ in golden characters,
    Eternally may shine.

———

THE INN.

 PILGRIM on his weary way
    Had plodded from the break of
    day ;
And now, when night was drawing on,
He felt his strength was almost gone ;
And looked around with anxious mind,
Hoping some resting-place to find.

And lo ! a castle with delight
He saw, upon a neighbouring height.
Then, mustering his remaining strength,
He reached the castle gate at length,
And begged, in words of simple grace,
To see the owner of the place.

His lordship came with haughty air,
And asked him what he wanted there.
The pilgrim made his meek request,—
A little food, a place of rest,—

The humblest bed, the meanest fare,
That might his failing strength repair.

The master listened with amaze;
Then, with a stern and angry gaze,
Said to the pilgrim : "Hence ! Away !
You cannot in my mansion stay.
This is no inn, where travellers rest ;
A little further make your quest."

The pilgrim turned, with look of pain,
But then addressed the lord again :
" Since here I may not find a friend,
To yonder hamlet I will wend ;
Yet I would fain three questions ask,
Ere I resume my toilsome task."

" Ask without fear," the lord replied,
" And answer shall not be denied."
" Pray," quoth the pilgrim, " tell me who
Dwelt in this castle before you ? "
" My father."   " Who before 'twas his ? "
" My ancestors for centuries."

" And tell me who," the pilgrim said,
" Will dwell here after you are dead ? "
" My son, I hope ; " the lord replied.
"Ah!" said the pilgrim,—and he sighed,—
" What is this but an inn, when they
Who dwell here make so short a stay ? "

His lordship paused, and mused a while ;
He looked no more with scornful smile.
" Alas ! " he said, " I sadly fear
" I've little known my duty here !
If this is but an inn, then I
To be a better host must try."

The pilgrim to his house he led,
And meat and wine before him spread ;
Then a soft silken couch he shows,
Whereon the pilgrim may repose ;
And rose next morn, at break of day,
To help his guest upon his way.

THE LILY AND THE PRIMROSE.

A FABLE.

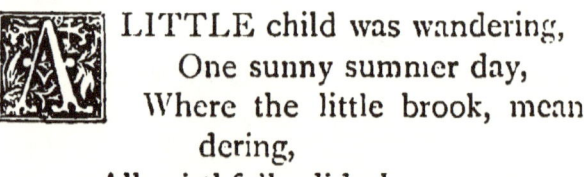

LITTLE child was wandering,
    One sunny summer day,
Where the little brook, mean-
    dering,
All mirthfully did play.

And while she thus was roving,
    She saw its golden crest,
A lily proud displaying,
    Above the brooklet's breast.

" How beauteous is this flower ! "
    The little child, she said ;
" How gorgeously doth tower
    Its lustrous golden head ! "

And then a primrose spying
    Upon the brooklet's side,
In grass half-hidden lying,
    All joyously she cried :

" But oh ! how far, far fairer
    Is this sweet little flower !
Sure ne'er was found a rarer
    In garden or in bower ! "

And straight with hand so loving
    She culled the primrose fair,
And placed it in her bosom ;
    But left the lily there.
1862.

* * *

THE POPPY AND THE DAISY.

A FABLE.

ITHIN a meadow, side by side,
    A poppy and a daisy grew ;
The poppy gay in gaudy pride,
    The daisy meekly hid from view

C

"Poor paltry thing," the poppy said,
"Why are thy thoughts so mean and low?
See how I boldly lift my head,
Whilst thou art cowering there below ! "

The daisy heard the scornful word ;
She heard, but did not make reply ;
For lo ! the thunder's roll was heard,
And clouds were gathering o'er the sky.

And soon the rain in torrents fell,
The storm beat fiercely everywhere ;—
The daisy from it sheltered well,
The poppy to its fury bare.

Soon was the furious tempest o'er,
The rainy flood had ceased to fall ;
The sun came from the clouds once more;
And golden sunshine covered all.

Then, while the poppy on the plain
Lay stretched along, all bruised and
     crushed,
The humble daisy bloomed again,
And with a sweeter beauty blushed.

THE WEEPING WILLOW.

A FABLE.

WEEPING willow grew by a
     brooklet's side,
     And overshadowed it from bank
to bank ;

But sadly swayed its branches in the
    breeze,
And drooping down sighed ceaselessly.
Then sang the nightingale.   All nature
    sat
Listening in silent rapture to the song.
" Ah ! " said the willow, when the strain
    was o'er,
" Why am not I a nightingale, that I
Such melodies might utter ? "

    A swan came swimming down the
    placid stream :
Its graceful form moved slowly on, and
    passed
Beneath the willow's branches, and at
    length
Was lost in the far distance.   Then the
    tree
Sighing again, exclaimed, " Ah ! would
    that I,
Like yon fair bird might float and gladden
    all
With grace and beauty ! "

    A noble horse went swiftly by, and bore
A warrior on his back.   With lightning
    speed
He flew, and from his hoofs the glowing
    sparks

Sprang upwards as he pass'd.   "Ah !"
    cried the tree,
"Why am not I a warrior's steed, to fly
Like lightning o'er the plain ?"

   High in the azure sky an eagle soared,
And higher and still higher flew, as tho'
He fain would reach the sun, whose burn-
    ing rays
His eye alone could meet with orb un-
    quenched.
Again the willow sighed, and sadly said :
" Were I an eagle too, how I would soar,
And make my dwelling-place above the
    clouds ! "

   The brooklet heard the willow's sighs,
    and paused
A moment in its course.   " O beauteous
    tree,"
It said, "cease, cease to sigh.   The good
    Creator
Hath blest His every creature ; and to
    thee
He gave surpassing beauty.   Cease to
    envy
The gifts of others ; for thine own are
    great."

The willow listened to the stream ; she
  gazed
Upon her beauteous form reflected fair
Within the watery mirror, and gazing still,
Forgot a while to sigh.

THE BREAD OF ST. JODOC.

A LEGEND.

O prove His servant came the
            Lord one day
      In meanest guise unto St.
  Jodoc's door,
And begged for bread.
            Unto the Almoner
The Abbot said : " Give to the wayfarer."
" Nay, master," said his servant ; " but
    one loaf
Is all remains."
          "Give," said the saint; "the Lord
Will see to us."

        The Almoner took the loaf,
And in four portions cut it. Turning then
Unto the beggar, " One for thee," he said,
" For me, the Abbot, and the dog, one
    each ! "

The Abbot heard and smiled.   The
   mendicant
Went on his way. In guise more woful still
Again the Lord came to St. Jodoc's door,
And begged an alms.
        " My portion give to him,"
The Abbot said. "The Lord will see to me."
The Almoner gave ; the beggar went his
   way.

Again with tattered garb and hungry looks
The Lord for alms begged at St. Jodoc's
   door.
"Give him thy portion," to the Almoner
The Abbot said ; "the Lord will see to
   thee."

The Almoner gave once more.   The
   beggar went.

But once again, lame, blind, half-naked
   came
The Lord and begged for bread.
        " Give the dog's portion,"
Then said the saint ; "the Lord will see
   to us."
The Almoner gave ; the beggar went his way ;
But as he went, a voice rang in their ears :
" Well done ! my faithful servant ; great
   thy faith ;

And, as thy faith, so thy reward shall be!"

And lo! as thro' the narrow window
    looked
The Almoner, along the river came
Four vessels sailing, all with viands full.
No man was there ; but on a pennon
    white
These words were writ : " The Lord, who
    feeds the ravens,
These vessels to His servant Jodoc sends,
Who, in one day, four times hath suc-
    coured Him :
One for the Abbot, for the Almoner one ;
One for the dog, one for the Giver's kin."

THE SISTERS.

AN ALLEGORY.

THE Almighty walked in Paradise,
    and came
    Where grew apart, in a most
beauteous garden,
The choicest blossoms of His love ; for
    these
Were they, who others, when on earth,
    had loved,
More than they loved themselves. And
    as He passed

Among the blossoms, these more brightly
    bloomed,
And sweeter odours cast around; and tones
Of wondrous symphonies filled all the air.

    Then came the Almighty to a spot re-
        tired,
And lo ! there yet was room for two.   A
    while
He gazed ; then to the attendant spirit
    turned,
And said : " Go swiftly thou to earth,
    where dwell
The children sad of Adam. Find me there
Two creatures worthy here to bloom, in
    this
The garden of my chief delight."

    Thro' space the spirit sped on swiftest
    wings,
And, like a falling star, on earth alighted.
Thro' many abodes of men he passed ;
    'mid scenes
Of sin and sorrow loving souls he found ;
But none of these were worthy deemed to
    blow
Within the garden of God's chief delight.

    At length, amid the dwellings of the
    poor,

The spirit entered one, most poor of all ;
And there, within the topmost attic, dwel
Two sisters.   One upon a bed of straw
Lay stretched, with scantiest covering
The cough, the hectic flush upon her
    cheeks,
Spoke of the approach of death.   The
    other sister
Knelt by her side.   Pale cheeks and hol-
    low eyes
Told the sad tale of want.

And then between the two arose a contest.
She who knelt press'd on her dying sister
The scanty remnants of their food.   "Take
    thou
The food, dear sister," then the sick one
    said,
"For thou hast greater need of it than I."
And neither sister could persuade the
    other.

The spirit gazed upon the scene, and said:
"Surely, ah, surely these are meet to
    blossom
In the Almighty's garden.   These I take."
    And when the kneeling one had risen,
    and crept
Close by her sister's side, while orisons sweet

Of resignation from their lips arose,
Soft sleep upon their eyelids shed the angel
Of Paradise ; and thro' their minds sweet
    dreams
Floated.   Together, so it seem'd to them,
They pass'd thro' air, and to a garden
    came,
Where flowers of fairest hue and fragrant
    odours
In myriads grew.   And then, it seem'd to
    them
They too were flowers, and bloom'd among
    the rest,
And sweetly smiled their sister flowers
    upon them.
While all the garden fair with dulcet voices,
That uttered wondrous harmonies, was fill'd,
In praise of Him Whose Presence was their
    life ;
And both the sisters join'd the joyous song.

    At morn, upon the straw, 'neath those
    poor rags,
Two sleeping forms were found, sleeping
    in death.
But gladdest smiles illumed the faces ;
    and,
To those who saw, it seem'd, as tho' from far,
Came fragrant odours and sweet melodies.

THE MERMAID.

AN ALLEGORY.

 SEA-GIRT isle, and nigh its
rocky shores
A troop of mermaids sporting.
Now here, now there, thro' the trans-
lucent waves
They swiftly darted in the full moon's
light.
But one, apart, 'neath an o'erhanging rock
Sat desolate, and gazed with fixèd eyes
Far thro' the moonlit waves.

A mermaid old
Approached. "Why art thou here," she said,
" While all thy fellows join in mirth and
sport ?
What grief so heavy weighs upon thy
heart ? "
" Because the time will come," the mer-
maid said,
" When I shall cease to be.   This form of
mine
Will fade away.   This spirit in the winds
Will be dissolved ; and I shall be as tho'
I ne'er had been at all.   This makes me
sad.
For this, I cannot join in sport and
laughter."

"Thou sayest the truth ; " replied the
    aged one ;
" But happier far than they of human race
Art thou and we.   Their life is but a span,
And full of pain and sickness.   Ours out-
    lasts
Their many generations ; and to us
Sickness and pain are things unknown."

" Nay," said the lone one ; " they of human
    race
Die not.   The body dies ; the spirit lives
For ever, and rejoices in its Maker.
Ah ! gladly would I bear the pain and
    sickness,
Could I, like man, possess a soul undying!"

" And know'st thou not," then said the
    aged one,
" Thou, too, mayst be like them ?   Hast
    thou ne'er heard,
The mermaid who for one of human race
Shall give her life, shall have a human soul,
And, like them, live for ever.   But life is
    sweet ;
And death is full of dread ; and never yet
Hath any of our race dared thus to pur-
    chase
A soul immortal."

The mermaid heard, and pondered.
    Shall she dare?
Shall she to the dear ocean bid adieu
And leave the liquid waves, the caves of
    crystal,
The tossing billows, all the mirth and sport?
Yea, she will dare. For tho' the mer-
    maid's life
Be glad and long, for her 'tis sadness, so
The thought of that last nothingness doth
    weigh
Upon her heart.

       Thro' the pellucid waves
Shone now the matutinal sunbeams. She
Rose from her seat under the crystal rock,
And hastened to approach the haunts of
    men.
Up the broad river swift she darts along.
The river narrows. Soon the o'erhanging
    trees
From bank to bank o'erarch the waters.
Then heard the mermaid children's joyous
    voices,
Shouts and glad laughter ; and she nearer
    drew
To where they played.

       One child she saw apart.

Upon the river's bank he stood and gazed
Upon a fish, that glittered in the sun-
    beams;
He stretched his hands, as tho' to grasp
    the creature;
He fell, and sank beneath the waters.
    Swift the mermaid
Sprang after him.   The current too was
    swift;
And far she darted, e'er she caught the
    child.
She bore him to the bank, and on the
    flowers,
That fringed the river, laid him.   His
    blue eyes
Were closed.   His locks hung heavy
    round his brow.
He spake not, moved not.   Lo ! the child
    was dead !

Soon rose the sound of sorrow.   O'er her
    child
The mother wept.   Beneath a willow's
    branches
That overhung the stream, the mermaid
    saw.
Then fill'd her heart a mighty resolution.
To the Creator lifting up her voice she
    cried:

"Take thou my life away; restore the
child's;
That so the sorrowing mother may rejoice!"

The Almighty heard her prayer. Closed
her eyes;
Her bosom ceased its beatings; on the
stream
Her lifeless body floated; but from beneath the willow,
Unseen by mortal eyes, sprang joyous upwards
A beauteous spirit, that, with arms outstretched,
And eyes intent aloft, flew heavenwards,
Winging with rapid flight to meet its
Maker.

—

THE DESERT ISLAND.

AN ALLEGORY.

 GENEROUS lord summoned
one day his slave,
And took him to the shore,
where lay at anchor
A noble ship, rich laden, and said to him:
'Lo! thou art free; this vessel, too, is
th ne.

Go, sail where'er thou wilt."
                         The slave, now free,
Thanked his good lord, then went on
  ᵒ board the ship,
And sailed away across the tranquil sea.
But lo ! at eve, a mighty tempest rose,
And drove the ship before it.   On a rock
It struck, and quickly sank beneath the
      waves.
Its master only out of all on board was
      saved,
And found himself, naked and helpless,
      lying
Upon a barren shore.   Hunger-press'd,
After long swoon he rose, and inland
      ventured,
Hoping to find shelter and food.   He
      reached a height ;
And lo ! in the far distance saw he then
A city fair, gilded by morning's sunbeams.
His steps he thither turned ; but e'er he
      came
Nigh to the city's gate, forth came a troop
With joyous acclamations; who, meeting
      him,
Bore him in triumph citywards.   They
      entered ;
And to a lordly palace bore him.   Royal
      robes

And golden crown they placed upon him,
    throned
In regal state : then bent the knee before
    him,
And hailed him king.
              " It is a dream," he said,
" A beauteous dream ; and I shall soon
    awake ! "
But days passed by, and still the dream
    continued ;
The shipwrecked outcast was indeed a
    king.

  At length, one day, wondering o'er these
    events,
He called an aged vizier, and enquired :
" Wherefore have ye, my subjects, chosen
    me
To be your king? How chancèd ye to know
That I upon your coast was cast?   Explain
This wondrous mystery."
             " Sire," said the vizier,
" In days long past, our ancestors remote
Made prayer to the Almighty, that each
    year
A monarch new might rule them.   Their
    prayer was heard.
Shipwrecked like thee, each year a stranger
    comes

Upon our shores, and him proclaim we
      king."
  "What do ye then with him who ruled
      before ? "
Enquired the king.
              "Alas ! his lot is hard ! "
The vizier answered.   " Borne unto the
      shore,
A little boat awaits him, and to a distant isle
Barren and desolate they carry him,
And leave him there."
              " And knew my predecessors
The fate that waited them ? "
                  " All of them knew ;
But all, enslaved by pleasure, spent their
      year
In folly, heedless of their destiny,
Till came the fatal day."
                  " Can naught avert
This dreadful doom ? " again enquired the
      king.
  "When comes the hour appointed,"
      said the vizier,
" Thou must depart ; such is thy destiny.
Yet if thou wisely use the year allotted,
Thou may'st prepare thyself a happy
      future."
  " I pray thee, tell me how ? " the king
      demanded.

"Thus," said the vizier; "in this thy
    year of rule
Send to thy future home, and build thy-
    self
A pleasant dwelling place. Thy subjects bid
To go and cultivate its barren soil ;
Bid gardens, woods and cities there ap-
    pear ;
Then, of thy subjects here, send thither
Those whom thou willest ; they will go
    with joy ;
And these shall be thy future subjects.
    When
The destined hour arrives, and thou from
    hence
Art borne upon the fatal bark, then these
Upon that other shore shall welcome thee,
And thou shalt reign for ever."

                  The king was wise.
The vizier's advice he followed carefully.
Artificers and husbandmen were sent ;
And soon the desert isle began to bloom
With trees and flowers ; a stately palace
    rose ;
And many a lovely cottage hid itself
'Neath sheltering trees ; and, as the year
    passed on,
Still fairer grew the isle, still wider spread

The fruits of prudent toil ; and gladly
    thither
Full many of his subjects went to dwell.

  The end approached.   The destined
    day arrived.
Stripped of his robes, his crown, the king
    was borne
Down to the shore, and there the boat
    stood ready.
Swiftly away they bore him. Soon the isle,
His destined home, was reached. The
    shore was filled
With joyous multitudes, to greet their
    king.
He landed midst acclaim; and royal robes,
And crown of gold, and throne of regal
    state,
Awaited him ; and there he reigned in
    bliss.

  And thou, O man, the shipwrecked
    outcast art,
The slave made free by a most bounteous
    lord.
To life naked and helpless cam'st thou ;
    king
Thou art ; thy subjects, all the gifts of
    God.

Thy reign is brief. Soon the bier shall
    bear thee
Across Death's ocean; but there awaits
    thy coming
A kingdom new, a long and happy reign,
If thou thy time on earth hast wisely
    spent.
Be prudent now. Prepare in time.
    Spend not
In folly and forgetfulness the fleeting
    hours;
Else, in long, dreary exile, shalt thou rue.

THE SCOFFER'S CONFESSION.

A TRUE STORY.

IT chanced, in one of France's
    greatest cities,
    A band of youths, who long the
hallowed path
Of Faith and Hope and Holiness had left,
One evening at the tavern spent their time,
In merriment together. Filled with wine,
Their childhood's pious teachings were
    their jest;
Things once deemed best and holiest now
    became

The objects of their laughter, until one,
More wanton than the rest, exclaimed :
  " 'Twere sport,
If one should to the priest his sins confess,
And all for mockery ! "
    Cried another then :
" I lay a wager, that the deed I do ! "
" Accepted ! " cried the first. " A dozen,
  I wage,
Of Champagne's choicest vintage you do
  not ! "
" Before the week has ended, I will go,"
The second said ; and all the room was
  filled
With laughter at the jest.
 Next noon the youth bethought him of
  his bet.
" I go ! " he said; "altho' the morning air
Makes things to wear a different aspect, yet
I go ; I will not lose the wager."
  'Tis eve ; and in the temple's dim-lit
  aisles
Behold the faithful gathered. One by one,
They enter the confessional's sacred shades,
And unto God, in person of his minister,
Open their hearts, with tears of penitence ;
And many a burthened soul lays down its
  load,
And goes away rejoicing.

One there came,
Upon whose face, had any looked, no signs
Of penitence were seen. The lip of scorn,
The mocking eye were his. Yet in his
    turn,
Where many more had entered, entered he;
And at the feet of him, of whom 'twas
    said :
" Whose sins thou shalt forgive, they are
    forgiven ;
Whose sins thou shalt retain, they are re-
    tained,"
The scorner knelt.
    " I come," he said, " my sins to tell ;
Yet not in penitence come I ; 'tis a jest ;
For I have laid a bet, and needs I win."
" Make thy confession then ; " the priest
    replied.
And lo ! the youth a history sad related
Of years spent in transgressions ; and as
    each sin
He told of that long, dreadful category,
The scornful words he added : " Naught
    care I ! "
Listened the holy priest in silent sadness ;
Yet in his heart he said : " The boy is
    mad !
Dear Lord, forgive ; and bring him back
    to Thee ! "

The long confession ended, said the
    priest :
" Now thou hast said thy say, unhappy
    boy,
I will say mine.   If thou wouldst win thy
    bet,
Thy task must be done wholly, not in part.
Confession made, comes penance ; and
    this is thine :
Three days, three times each day, morn,
    noon, and eve,
Upon thy knees these words I bid thee
    say :
' Death follows life ; but naught I care for
    death ;
Then judgment comes ; for judgment
    naught I care ;
Last cometh hell ; but naught I care for
    that ! '
Such is thy penance ; look thou do it well !"

The youth departed. Soon, with laughter
    wild,
His comrades heard.   "Do thou the pen-
    ance," cried they,
" Else losest thou the bet."   " The bet I
    lose not,"
Answered the youth.   " The penance I
    will do."

And morn, and noon, and evening, he
    knelt,
And said the penance that was laid upon
    him :
" Death follows life ; but naught I care
    for death ;
Then judgment comes ; for judgment
    naught care I ;
Last cometh hell ; but naught I care for
    hell ! "

First from his lips the words came care-
    lessly ;
But, as he said, back to his spirit came
The sweet remembrances of days gone by,
When at a mother's knee he knelt, and
    learned
To pray ; and as the dreadful sentences
Fell from his tongue, his soul was filled
    with horror.
" Death, judgment, hell ! " he scarce had
    heart to utter
The awful words. " Care not for these ! "
    he said ;
"I needs must care : 'twere madness else;"
    and ere
The penance was complete, the three days
    passed,
Again the holy priest beheld the youth,

Not now in mockery kneeling, but with
    tears
Of penitence unfeigned. And soon he
    rose,
The band of scoffers ne'er to meet again.

CASTLES IN THE AIR.

NOW I do love, in the still hour of
    eve,
    After the sun hath sunk down
in the west,
When sleeps the day-bird in its downy nest,
My books and studies for awhile to leave,
And slowly stray, in thoughtful mood, and
    muse,
In my own thoughts shut up, on many a
    theme ;
Or for the future build fair hopes, that
    seem,
In the far distance lying, clothed in hues
Of fairy splendour, or which glowing shine
Like joys of some sweet earthly paradise,
Painted by fancy as entirely mine.
And tho' in sober thought I well perceive,
That hopes like these will never greet
    mine eyes,
Yet still I love them, and great joy they
    give.
    1862.

UNREST.

O H ! could thy soul but leave its
high aspiring,
And, like the multitude, con-
tented be
To pass day after day unceasingly
In the same changeless round ; if no
desiring
Of higher, nobler things, thy bosom firing
With restless longings, eager to pursue
Some aim sublime, that mocks thy
eager view,
Now in thy changeful breast fair hope
inspiring,
Now plunging deep thy soul in black
despair,
Then cheating thee again with kindlier
smiling,
Again thy brightening hopes away to
tear,
With cruel hand—perchance without a care
Of higher things, thou might'st, thy time
bewhiling
With petty things, not then these achings
bear.

1867.

THE SHORTNESS OF LIFE.

SEE, when the morning sun doth
        gild the sky,
    The flow'ret blooms in his en-
livening streams,
It opes, it spreads its bosom to his beams,
With fragrant breath and beauty-glowing
    eye.
But soon the morn, the noon have passèd
    by,
Night cometh on, and as it comes, so
    fades
The flow'ret, withered ere the evening
    shades
Have fairly come;—so soon the flower
    doth die.
Lo! such is man! Short as the flower's
    his day!
He cometh, and the hours, days, years
    pass on,
And quickly bear him from this bourne
    away;
Till soon his little span of life is o'er—
Fled like the shades,—his short existence
    gone,
And but an empty name remains,—no
    more.
    1868.

TO THE OCEAN.

RUSH, rush, thou ever-shifting
ocean, on,—
Rush, dashing, splashing on the
sand-strewn shore !
Ye depths unseen in your dark caverns
moan,
Ye mighty, never-resting billows roar !
Unfathomed, measureless, immense, pro-
found,
That with thy hundred arms, Briareus
like,
Dost span the earth in close embrace
around,
And now with furious rage dost terror
strike
Into her, now play round her like a child
In wanton merriment, with many a soft
caress ;
Wondrous art thou, whether with aspect
wild
Thou rage sublime, in awful restlessness,
Or the glad sunshine on thy brow serene
Doth spread in quiet splendour all his
golden sheen.

1867.

TO ERIN.

FAIR ocean Isle, two winters now are thine.
The one hath robb'd thy mountains and thy vales
Of thy green verdure; driven, with wintry gales,
The joyous songsters from thy groves, to find
Welcome in other lands; the leaves and flowers
Withered from trees and meadows, and left bare
Thy whilom lovely aspect. Fiercer far
That other winter which still grimly glowers,
And long hath glower'd upon thee. Cruel might,
And savage tyranny, with rancorous hate,
Have made thy once blest homesteads desolate,
And filled thee all with horror and affright.
But soon shall both these winters cease their reign,
And twofold spring-time make thee smile again.

The icy north shall its rude blasts recall ;
Again the woodland quirists their sweet
    song
Shall raise thy hills and meadowlands
    among—
And kindly rain and sunshine cover all
Thy land with leaf and flower. Gay
    shall be
Thy aspect then, sweet Erin. The harsh
    reign
Of withering tyranny that long hath lain,
Filling thee with dismay and death, shall
    see
Its speedy end ; and from thy every shore
Shall smile prosperity and glad content ;
While all thy virtues, like sweet flowers,
    shall scent
The air with fragrant perfumes : and no
    more
Thy loving sons, exilèd far from thee,
Shall with vain longing pine their father-
    land to see.
    1868.   ——

ROME.

DEAD is the city of proud memo-
    ries !
    Dead is the city of the ancient
    date !
Pass'd are her days of glory and of state.

Ended at last are her high destinies !
City of kings, city of heroes, is
Thy doom at length spoke by the mouth
    of fate?
Shall fame no more upon thy borders
    wait?
Glory no more recount thy victories?
Rome, city of kings and martyrs, is not
    dead.
Foes and false friends are eager to betray,
Foes and false friends shall soon be
    scatterèd.
City of Pontiffs, thou shalt ne'er decay
Till the great world itself shall bow its
    head,
And sun and moon and stars shall pass
    away.
   1870.

———

THE VOYAGE BEGUN.

 LITTLE wail announced thine
        advent here,
      Into a world which is a world
of wail,
 A new adventurer on this sea to sail,
To sound its shallow joys, thy bark to
    steer
Over its woes profound.   O world of fear !

O ocean wondrous we are sailing o'er,
Each after other venturing from the
shore
Upon its unknown waters! Ocean drear,
How can we venture on thy waves
alone?
How can we venture our frail tottering
boat
Midst dreadful storms and cheating calms
to float,
Midst quicksands and alluring rocks,
unknown—
We weak, unskilful, timorous creatures
prone
To be deceived, unknowing, without
thought?
1869.

———

THE MYSTERY OF THE TRINITY.

ALONG the shore of the deep-
sounding sea
The sage of Hippo paced, in
mighty thought;
For, as he upward gazed, his spirit sought,
With eager yearning, the great mystery
To fathom of the wondrous One-in-Three.
Vainly he strove; no ray, with brightness
fraught,

E

The longed-for image to his vision brought,
That might explain how such strange
    thing could be.
And lo ! a child upon the strand, who
    sought,
With ocean's waves, to fill a hollow
    small !
Then said the saint : " And think'st thou,
    child, that all
This ocean vast may in thy trench be
    brought ? "
" And think'st thou," said the child, with
    smile of light,
" That mortal mind can grasp the In-
    finite ? "

———

THE FIRE OF LOVE.

A LEGEND OF ST. WENCESLAS.

'TWAS the chill winter. On the
    frozen ground,
    The trees, the cottage roofs,
thick lay the snow
And heavy. The piercing storm-gusts
    blow
Across the plain. To yonder cottage
    bound,

Behold, with hasty step, the royal saint,
His shoulders laden with a weighty store
Of fuel for its inmates, hurries o'er
The snow; and after him a boy, now faint
With cold. "My master dear, I can no more!
My limbs are stiff; my very heart is chill'd!"
Then said the saint, his breast with pity fill'd;
"Tread in my footsteps, child, who go before."
The boy obeyed. Love's fire divine, that press'd
E'en from his master's footsteps, warmed his breast.

ST. CADOC'S CLOAK.

"O, bring me fire; I needs must bake to-day;"
    The hermit Meuthi to his pupil said.
Unto the threshing-floor straight Cadoc sped,
Where Tidys with the flail was busy. "Stay,

O Tidys, from thy toil awhile.   For fire
I come from holy Meuthi," said the boy.
" Fire dost thou want ? I have no time to
 toy ;
Go ; elsewhere seek the thing that ye re-
 quire.
Yet stay ; I give thee fire ; but thou must
 take
The embers in that cloak of thine ;
 naught
I give thee else, even for Meuthi's sake."
The embers in his mantle Cadoc caught,
And with all haste unto his master came ;
And lo ! the cloak was scathcless from
 the flame.

———

ST. CADOC AND THE MOUSE.

O Brecknock once St. Cadoc
 came, to learn
 From Bachan's lips ; and lo !
in all the land
Was famine sorc.   The poor on every
 hand
Clamour for bread ; and to St. Cadoc
 turn
Their tearful eyes for comfort.   Burns
 his breast

With pity.   Unto God with tears he
    prays :
"O Thou, Whose hand the raven's hunger
    stays,
Succour Thy children, now so sore dis-
    tress'd ! "
And lo ! a mouse, with artful wile and
    play,
Brings to the saint a single grain of wheat,
Lays it before him, and then turns away.
Follows the saint, with no unwilling feet.
It leads him where a hidden granary lay,
With store of corn well-filled, wholesome
    and sweet.

ST. ILLTYD AND THE STAG.

ILD Merchion with his dogs the
    stag pursued
      O'er Llantwit's brakes and
marshes.   Swift in flight
Sped on the beast, till came it where the
    knight,
St. Illtyd, dwelt alone in desert rude.
Into the hermit's cell, for refuge, bounds
The wearied stag, hard by the blood-
    hounds press'd,
And on the ground it lies in trustful rest ;

While spell-bound at the portal stand the
   hounds.
The eager huntsmen come, and with
   amaze
On stag reposing on the cottage floor,
The panting blood-hounds standing at the
   door,
The holy hermit in the midst, they gaze.
Of higher justice Merchion owns the
   sway ;
He leaves the stag, and calls his hounds
   away.

———

ST. SAMSON AND THE MEAD-CASKS.

THE poor came crowding round
   the Convent gate,
   By hunger driven.   Samson
with lavish hand
The Convent's stores among the famished
   band
Divided, corn and mead.   With hearts
   elate,
Their hunger satisfied, they blessed the
   saint,
And went their way ; the saint went to his
   books.

At noontide hour the monks, with angry
    looks,
Unto the abbot came, and made com-
    plaint.
Samson the mead had wasted; none was
    left
To place upon the noontide table.
    Straight
The abbot views the mead-casks. Sadly
    wait
The thirsty monks, of wonted cheer be-
    reft.
Samson is called. He comes. The
    holy sign
He makes. The empty casks are filled
    with wine.

THE VOCATION OF ST. ISSYLIO.

ISSYLIO with his brothers in the
    wood,
    Pursued the forest denizens;
when lo!
A band of monks passed by. Solemn and
    slow
They went, singing sweet hymns. Issylio
    stood

And listened to the strains. The har-
    mony fills
The woodland glades. Cease the birds'
    sweet notes,
While on the air that sweeter music floats,
Which thoughts of Heaven into the breast
    instils.
Pass'd the procession, straight Issylio
    said :
" Lo ! I the chase abandon, home, and
    all !
These heavenly voices to my spirit call,
And needs I follow whither I am led."
The world abandoning, with the monks
    he went,
And in God's service all his years were
    spent.

———

HOLY OBEDIENCE.

THE monk in the scriptorium sat
    and wrote
    The Gospel. Line by line and
stroke by stroke
Slowly he traced the holy characters,
    which spoke
Of Him, whom Love Divine from Heaven
    had brought

To take upon Himself the form of man,
And, mortal, dwell with mortals,—of his
    life,
His holy teaching, and His ceaseless
    strife
With human sin and sorrow ; and, as ran
His quill along, the monk in deepest
    thought
Was wholly wrapt,—entranced his spirit so
The wondrous mysteries, that the writing
    taught.
The final letter of God's name he made ;
And lo ! 'twas said : " The Abbot calls
    thee ; go ! "
He left the stroke unfinished, and obeyed.

———

THE VENERABLE PHILIP EVANS AND HIS HARP.*

 Harp of Cymru, never with
    sweeter swell
    Didst utter song than then,
when he, to whom
'Twas said : " At morn thou meetest a
    felon's doom,"

* The V. Philip Evans died for his religion at
Cardiff on July 22nd, 1679. On being told,
while amusing himself one day at a game of
bowls in the Castle grounds, that he was to die
the next morning, he said : " What hurry ! Let
us finish our game." Having done so, he was so

Awoke thy chords to sing his last farewell !
That felon's death the martyr dreaded not ;
For well he knew that he was doomed to
    die,
Because that he, like them of days gone
    by,
The hand that blessed, the gifted tongue
    had got.
O Saints of Cymru, David, Teilo, thou
Llancarvan's sage, and thou, famed
    Llantwit's knight,
With all the rest, who sweeter incense
    light,
To burn before that Greater Altar now,
Oh ! plead with God, your children's
    offspring may,
Like them of old, soon learn the Better
    Way.

THE DONKEY TURNED FLUTIST.

FROM THE SPANISH OF YRIARTE.

HIS same little fable,
    Like you it, or not,
    I have this moment thought of
    y chance.

full of joy, that he took up his harp, on which he
was an accomplished player, and spent some time
in playing upon it his favourite airs.

Round about some meadows,
That lie near my abode,
Wandered one day a donkey
  By chance.

A flute within those meadows
He found ; some country lout
Had left it there,—forgotten
  By chance.

Of course our noble donkey
Must smell what it was like,
And at that moment snorted
  By chance.

And through the flute his snorting
An impulse chanced to send ;
And then, the flute it sounded
  By chance.

" Oh ! " cried our noble donkey,
" Who says I cannot play ?
Yet some will blame my music,
  Perchance ! "

Of rules of art unknowing
There many donkeys are,
Who *once* are *quite* successful,
  By chance.

THE POET AND THE SEA.

FROM THE GREEK OF MOSCHUS.

WHEN softly moves the wind across
the wave,
My timid mind is stirred,—the
Muse no more
Doth please ; I stand delighted on the
shore.
But when the grisly depths of ocean rave,
And foaming surge, and mighty billows
fling,—
Then to the land I turn, and shun the
seas,
And earth seems trusty, and the dim
woods please,—
Where though the gale blow, sweet the
pine doth sing.
An evil life the fisherman hath wed,—
His bark his home, his toil upon the sea,
The doubtful winnings of the net his
bread !
For me,—I love to slumber 'neath a
shady tree,
A brooklet murmuring near my rustic
bed,
Whose sounds delightful never bid me
flee.

THE LIFE OF MAN.

FROM THE GREEK OF MININERMUS.

WE, like the leaves at flow'ry hour
        of Spring
    Brought forth, when sudden shines the fiery sun
With hotter glow, the blossomed days of
    youth
Awhile enjoy, careless alike of good,
Careless of ill.   But round our path black
    Cares
Have ta'en their stand.   The one hath in
    her hand
Eld's lonesome lot, and Death her sister
    holds.
A little span Youth's joys endure, while
    lasts
The sunny Spring.   But when the glowing
    hour
Hath pass'd away, far better 'twere, me-
    thinks,
That Death should come forthwith.   For
    many an ill,
From household cares and poverty's sad
    lot,
The life of man molests.   One fondly
    yearns

For children's loving smile, yet dies un-
　　wept
By son or daughter dear; worn by disease,
Another lingers on; nor is there mortal
　　man,
Who at the hand of Zeus receives not
　　many an ill.

———

THE PLACE OF REST.

FROM THE FRENCH OF PORCHAT.

YONDER below, the hamlet nigh,
　　Around that black tower doth it
　　lie ;
Beneath the elm, whose foliage green
Rustleth in the breeze of e'en.
'Tis there our miseries shall cease,
'Tis there our fathers rest in peace ;
Till comes the great awakening cry,
Sweet sleep there on our eyes shall lie.

Behold the turf uneven lies ;
As ocean's billows fall and rise,
So mounds and hollows small and great
In this enclosure alternate ;
And flowers in countless numbers grace
The spot, where once a tomb found plac..
Till comes the great awakening cry,
Sweet sleep there on our eyes shall lie.

GO, PRAY.

FROM THE FRENCH OF VICTOR HUGO.

O, pray. It is the eve—the still,
  soft eve ;
  The twilight cometh on—the
night is nigh.
It is the hour when earthly feelings leave
The soul awhile. With holy thoughts and
  high
Aspirings doth the subdued spirit heave :
Go, while these feelings move thee ; raise
  thine eye,
      And pray.

The sun is setting on the horizon low ;
His last bright beams across the welkin
  stealing
Are shedding there a softer, purer glow,
Like the remembrance of some bye-gone
  feeling :
Go ; turn thee to thy God, go to thy
  chamber now,
While the soft inspiration's on thee, kneel-
  ing
      To pray.

Go, pray. For whom? For what? There
  is around
A world in woe,—a race of millions dying

In sin, in misery,—thoughtless, careless,
    drowned
In vice and wretchedness and want, yet
    lying
Unknowing of their woe. Oh! gaze
    around !
For these upraise thine eyes to heaven,
    sighing,
                        And pray.

Oh ! pray with heart and mind and soul ;
    and naught
But thy petition feeling, in that hour
Forget all else. Yea, let not e'en a thought,
But thy great prayer unto the Father—our
Great Father—rise within thy mind.   He
    taught
His children prayer,—then go with power,
                        And pray.

Pray for the wicked man,—the man of sin ;
O pray for him with heaving, anxious
    breast ;
And bid the tears of sorrow, pent within
Thine eyes, flow down with sympathy ;
    and rest
Not, cease not, till thy mighty pleading.
    win
The ear of Him, Who bade us, when on
    earth a guest,
                        To pray.

Remember, Oh! remember, over him,
When lying lisping on a mother's knee,
Fond eyes have gazed, filled up to the
    brim
With tears, with tears of love; remember he
Was once a fair, sweet, loving child,—tho'
    grim
His spirit now with guilt and misery;—
                And pray.

E'en now, perchance, at times a vision o'er
His spirit comes,—a dream of byegone
    years;
And he looks back upon the time once
    more,
When at a mother's knee he prayed. The
    tears,
Hot, scalding, trickle down,—his head,
    now hoar
With years, bows grief-struck, as again he
    hears
                Her pray.

And there are those who never had a
    mother
Who taught them in their infancy to kneel
And pray; who never prayed for self or
    other;
Remember these to Him, whose balm can
    heal
                         F

The vilest; for each of them is still thy
    brother,
Though black.　Remember these, and for
    their weal,
          Go, pray !

The sun is set, the twilight deepens, and
A stilly hush broods over all.　The eve
Is tranquil,—meet for prayer ; and soft
    and bland
The breeze flows on; the dying light doth
    weave
Shades dark and darker now on every
    hand.
All, all is peace around.　Hasten, ere it
    leave,
          And pray.

Pray for the weeper, who within the tomb
Hath placed her best-beloved ; for him
    who mourns
Over his dearest.　All is dark, dark gloom
For them.　Their hopes dashed from
    them, oh, how burns
The anguish-stricken heart, and torpor
    dumb
Seizes upon them !　For these, while yet
    thy spirit yearns,
          Go, pray.

The widow and the orphan,—pray for
    them.
Forget them not ! Unhappy they, be-
    reaved
Of him, who was their stay ; now left to
    stem
The world's rough tide alone! They had
    believed
That many happy years awaited him ;
And suddenly they woke to woe, too
    grieved
                To pray.

'Tis night. The sky is veiled in darkness.
    Lo !
The moon shines softly as she strays along.
Above, the stars gleam quietly. Below,
The birds are silent in their nests. The
    song
Of insects too is hush'd. The rustling
    low
Of leaves alone is heard. Think it not
    long !
              Still pray !

THE BEE.

A FABLE.

FROM THE GERMAN.

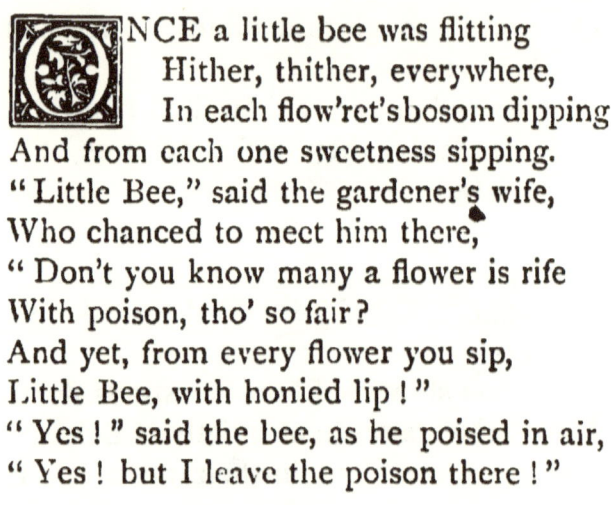

ONCE a little bee was flitting
Hither, thither, everywhere,
In each flow'ret's bosom dipping
And from each one sweetness sipping.
"Little Bee," said the gardener's wife,
Who chanced to meet him there,
"Don't you know many a flower is rife
With poison, tho' so fair?
And yet, from every flower you sip,
Little Bee, with honied lip!"
"Yes!" said the bee, as he poised in air,
"Yes! but I leave the poison there!"

WHEN THE SWALLOWS HOME-
WARD FLY.

FROM THE GERMAN.

WHEN the swallows homeward fly,
When the roses fade and die,
When the nightingale's sweet song
With the nightingale is gone,

Asks my heart, with bitter smart,
If I thee shall see again,—
Parting, ah, parting is such pain !

When the swans all southward go,
Thither where the citrons blow ;
When the evening glory fades,
Glancing thro' the wood's dim shades,
Asks my heart, with bitter smart,
If I thee shall see again,—
Parting, ah, parting is such pain !

Why, poor heart, so sore distrest ?
Thou at last shalt also rest.
What on earth is doomed to die,
Shall we see again on high ?
Asks my heart, with bitter smart.
Yes, we all shall meet again,
Although the parting is such pain !

———

THE CATHEDRAL OF COLOGNE.

FROM THE GERMAN.

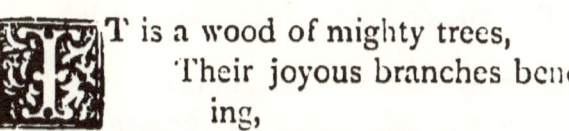

T is a wood of mighty trees,
        Their joyous branches bend-
            ing,
And from them pious thoughts like birds
    To Heaven are e'er ascending.

The hardy thought, the earnest striving,
  That made these stones like flowers to
      blow ;
Such was our fathers' life and nature,
  Now found no more on earth below.

Thus do these lofty pillars speak,
  That ever heavenward draw our gaze ;
Between which, as in shady groves,
  The pious suppliant kneels and prays.

And where the soul its secret tells,
  In silent, shady, holy light,
A tapestry is overhung,—
  A tent with saintly pictures bright.

Upon those variegated panes
  It is no idle light that gleams ;
'Tis a reflection earthward falling
  Of endless joys which on them beams.

But sideways, sweetest spot, thou draw'st
      me ;
  To thee my ardent longings swell,
Chapel, wherein with love and mercy
  The ancient faith doth ever dwell.

Here may no noisy songs arise,
  Although with songs my bosom beats ;
But silently, where angels sing,
  Mary's sweet smile my spirit greets.

THE POOR FIDDLER.

A LEGEND.

T Mentz, in ages distant,
 A fiddler poor, and old,
  With hoary hair and tattered
 rags
Was beggin in the cold.

Alas ! how cold and hungry,
 How faint I am and weak !
Will no one have some pity,
 And grant the aid I seek ?

I once was young and happy ;
 I sang with power then,
And my fiddle, by its sweetness,
 Entranced the ears of men.

But now, poor, old, and lonely,
 My singing days long gone—
They say :—" Come, tune thy fiddle,
 And sing, thou aged one ! "

At Mentz, along the river,
 The old man walked distressed ;
Till he came to a little chapel
 Where he stopped to pray and rest.

And, stepping within the doorway,
  On an altar he doth behold
The Holy Virgin's image,
  Gleaming in silk and gold.

With prayerful eyes upgazing,
  From her he seeks relief;
And it seemed as though her gentle voice
  Soothèd the old man's grief.

Then from his eyes, for gladness,
  The tears in torrents pressed;
And before her image, to thank her,
  He played his very best.

He played and sang before her:
  "Thou knewest want's bitter smart;
And thou hearest not my fiddle,
  But thou seest my grateful heart."

And when the song was ended,
  And as he turned away,
The image threw a slipper of gold
  For his tune and song to pay.

The old man seized the slipper,
  He kissed it o'er and o'er;
And then with haste to the city went,
  For hunger pressed him sore.

But the watchman chanced to see him,
   As he hastened off with glee ;
And "Hold !" he cried, "thou wicked
    thief ;
   That slipper give to me ! "

" 'Twas the holy image gave it,
   For my tune and song to pay,"
He said ; but the people laughed,
   And they led him quick away.

And as, along the pathway,
   He passed the chapel door,
He stood before the image,
   And prayed, as he did before.

" Thyself hast known much sorrow,
   Thyself hadst woes to bear ;
To thee I offer my poor old heart,
   Ah ! take it in thy care !"

And again the aged fiddler
   Placed his fiddle against his breast,
And he sang before the image,
   And played his very best.

And when the song was ended,
   And as he turned away,
Another slipper the image threw,
   For his tune and song to pay.

The people gazed with wonder,
 And they cried aloud with fear ;
" 'Twas the Holy Virgin gave them,
 And God is surely here ! "

They all kneel down in sorrow,
 And each one humbly prays,
And then, with the aged fiddler,
 They sing the Virgin's praise.

———

THE TAILOR OF BRABANT.

FROM THE GERMAN.

THE wine that's best for children
  Is that clear wine which flows
 Down from the rock-girt foun-
tain,
 And carols as it goes.

It flows through verdant meadows,
 It flows through bush and brake ;
And bird and beast all drink it,
 For it makes no head to ache.

And if this wine for children
 Is the best that they can drink,
To their elders it would do no harm,
 If they drank it too, I think,

In Brabant there was a tailor,—
    His name I cannot tell,—
But he drank not much of the white wine,
    This I know, alas, full well.

Our tailor's choice was the red wine,
    He loved it exceedingly ;
He drank so much of the red wine,
    That his head hung heavily.

Then, the sport of all naughty children,
    He tottered on his way,
Until in the midst of the market place
    The drunken tailor lay.

And while there he lay and slumbered,
    As drunk as drunk could be,
There passed that way Count Philip,
    The Lord of Burgundy.

He pressed through the crowd of gazers
    To see what was lying there ;
And he bade them to the castle
    The drunken tailor bear.

Then spake Count Philip, laughing,
    For his heart beat merrily :
" I' faith, the tailor's punishment
    Our pastime now shall be."

And in the Count's richest garments,
    Silk robe and golden vest,
With coronet and ribands gay,
    The sleeping man they dressed.

And, when his sleep was over,
    They cried, on bended knee :
"All Hail, our liege, Count Philip,
    The Lord of Burgundy!"

Our tailor rubbed his eyelids,
    He rubbed them o'er and o'er ;
He listened, and he listened,
    And they shouted as before.

He gazed with joy and wonder
    On gold and precious stone,—
On his coronet of glittering pearls,
    And on his ivory throne.

As Count he heard them greet him,
    He saw the lighted hall,
His ears they heard, his eyes beheld,
    And it vexed him not at all.

The honours and the glory,
    They pleased him mightily ;
"Doubtless I am Count Philip
    The Lord of Burgundy!"

First timidly, then boldly,
　He issues his command;
First with the smile of favour,
　Then with the threatening hand.

To do his will the servants
　Are hurrying here and there;
Not the Count himself e'er bore him
　With such a lordly air.

At last he cried with anger:
　" Make haste, you lazy lot;
For a draught of wine I'm parching,
　And yet you bring it not.

" And hark ye, bring the red wine;
　For, by my coronet,
That horrid stuff, your white wine,
　I loved it never yet."

And then the huge golden goblet
　He drained full thirstily;
And sleep once more o'ermastered
　The Count of Burgundy.

As Count Philip of Burgundy
　In the Castle he fell asleep;
But, as tailor, in the market-place,
　He awoke from slumber deep.

He called upon his servants ;—
  With threatening words he said :
" Bring not to me your white wine,—
  I only drink the red."

But instead of a velvet cushion,
  On the cold, hard stone he lies ;
And near him, in the fountain,
  The cool, white wine he spies.

And the tailor, parched and thirsty,
  Of that hated wine did drink,
And then, with sober footsteps,
  Homeward began to slink.

But, as he tottered onward,
  The crowd cried scoffingly :
" All Hail, our liege, Count Philip,
  The Lord of Burgundy ! "

And the tailor never after
  From his dwelling ventured out,
But the scornful crowd would follow
  With mocking laugh and shout.

Now lest you too should suffer
  The tailor's cruel fate,
Be sure you do not learn, like him,
  The pure white wine to hate.

THE ERL-KING.

FROM THE GERMAN OF GOETHE.

HO rideth so late through the
night so wild?
It is the father with his child.
He holdeth the boy close in his arm;
He grasps him tightly, he keeps him
warm.

" My son, why hidest thy face with fear?"
" Seest not, father, the Erl-king near?—
The Erl-king, with his crown and train?"
" My son, 'tis a mist athwart the plain."

" My darling child, come, go with me,
And gladsome games will I play with thee.
Fair are the flowers on our sea-side path,
And garments of gold my mother hath."

" My father, my father, and dost thou not
hear,
What Erl-king whispereth soft in mine
ear?"
" Be quiet, rest thee quiet, my child;
The branches rustle in the night-wind
wild."

" Wilt, pretty child, thou not come with
    me ?
My daughters shall wait on thee fair and
    free ;
My daughters the nightly dance shall
    keep,—
They shall dance and sing and rock thee
    to sleep."

" My father, my father, and seest thou
    not
Erl-king's daughters in yon shady spot ? "
' My son, my son, I see it full well ;—
'Tis the mist on the meadows worketh the
    spell."

" I love thee, I love thee, thou beauteous
    boy;
And, art thou not willing, must force em-
    ploy ! "
" My father, my father, he seizeth me now ;
Ah ! Erl-king hath done me a hurt, I
    trow ! "

The father shudders ; fast rideth he on ;
He holds in his arms his moaning son ;
He reacheth his home with fear and
    dread ;
Within his arms his child lay dead.

THE OLD GENERAL.

FROM THE GERMAN OF CANON SCHMIDT.

EAR children, listen to my song :
    There lived upon his pension
    A general, now no longer
young,—
A man of high intention ;
To help, to console, to gladden, to give,
For this alone he seemed to live.

His son had died, and he, beguiled,
    Adopted as his daughter,
From kindliness, his sister's child,—
    A pious girl he thought her ;
But she loved only gold, and pearls, and
    rings,
And other such transient, worldly things.

" Child," said the general one day,
    "You give me little pleasure ;
You care for naught but dress and play,
    And the poor you do not treasure ;
I am aging fast, and must soon depart :
Would you be my heiress, amend your heart.

" And now, I go awhile from home ;
    But I leave you money in plenty,
That, when to my door the poor shall come,
    They never may go away empty ;
And if ever a soldier comes, poor and old,
Give him, for my sake, a ducat of gold."

G

He goes.   Night comes.   She hears a rap;
   And at the door discovers
An aged soldier, whose bear-skin cap
   His countenance quite covers;
On his crutches he feebly totters nigh,
And begs for a little charity.

" You   drunken   knave," exclaimed   the
      shrew,
   " A little further crutch it !
My money's not for such as you,
   And you shall never touch it ;
Pack off, you shameless, drunken thief,
Or   my   dog   shall   bring   your   shins   to
      grief."

" Is it thus you do my will ? " he cried ;
   And, aside his bear-skin throwing,
She saw the general by her side,
   His eyes like lightning glowing.
" 'Twas my wish to fairly test your heart,—
And now, from my house, you must de-
      part.

" You cannot now my heiress be ;
   Pack off, without delaying.
You need not cry and pray to me ;
   My house you shall not stay in.
For a girl who drives the poor away,
Need never to an old soldier pray."

THE RAIN-DROP.

FROM THE GERMAN OF CANON SCHMIDT.

 SUDDEN shower, one April day,
Disturbed three children at
their play ;
And soon the nimble youngsters stood
'Neath shelter of a neighb'ring wood.

Scarce had the rain-drops ceased to patter,
Scarce had the sun begun to scatter
His rays again, when something bright
Fell on the children's wondering sight.

"Oh ! what a lovely light is this ! "
Cried Charles ; " just look how bright it is !
See, Fred'rick, in the bush ; its hue—
I never saw so clear a blue."

" I see the little light," cried Fred,
"There, on the branch above my head ;
But yet—I'm sure—what can you mean ?
I never saw a brighter green."

"Green, blue," cried Hal ; "where are
your eyes ?
The tiny light close by me lies ;
And, I declare, it is as red
A light as ever ruby shed."

The lads returnèd to their play.
Whence was that many-coloured ray?
A rain-drop there reflected bright
A sunbeam to the children's sight.

Thus oft unto our earnest eyes
The truth in varied colour lies;
But when we get a nearer view,
We see one pure, unchanging hue.

———

THE BOOK WITHOUT LETTERS.

FROM THE GERMAN OF CANON SCHMIDT.

 PEASANT, at his cottage door,
A little book was reading o'er,—
A simple, untaught, aged man,
Whose locks in silvery tresses ran;
His cheeks, of rosy colour yet,
With quickly dropping tears were wet.

A doctor, with each, science pat,
Beheld the peasant as he sat;
Though learned and of high repute,
He bent, the peasant to salute;
" Old simpleton, now tell me, pray,
Do you e'en know the letter A ? "

" Nor letter A, nor letter B,
Sir Doctor, e'er was known to me ;
Nor does my little book contain
Aught but six empty pages plain ;
Six too the tints those pages hold ;—
Now list the truths those tints unfold.

" The first, of heaven's bright blue, doth
    say,
Mine eyes should heavenward ever stray :
The next, whose hue with roses vies,
Tells of the blood that purifies ;
The third's clear whiteness says to me,
' Seek thou the lily's purity.'

" The fourth, which bears night's dark-
    some hue,
Tells me that death to all is due ;
The fifth, with fiery coloured glare,
Seems with the gleam of hell to stare ;
While the sixth page, with golden light,
Pictures to me heaven's glorious sight.

" When on these simple truths I pore,
My heart is stirred, the tears run o'er ;
I find here all I need to know ;
And all the tomes your shelves can show,
Volumes on volumes, rich and rare,
Cannot with this my book compare."

Sir Doctor stood, and thought a minute.
" H'm," he exclaimed, " there's something
     in it.
Who little does, though much he know,
Far from the mark will surely go ;
Who little knows, but does it too,
Is wise as well as good and true."

THE WOODCUTTER.

FROM THE GERMAN OF CANON SCHMIDT.

PEASANT was felling a knotty
     oak ;
     He sighed and murmured at
every stroke.
" What endless sorrow, what ceaseless pain
It costs a poor man's bread to gain !
Alas ! Alas ! 'Tis a wretched fate !
Would God I'd been born of rich estate !"

And lo ! a beautiful youth stood at hand,
With silver garments and golden wand ;
He spoke to the peasant in kindly tone,
"God bless you, you poor unfortunate one!
Whatever you wish, ask without any dread ;
Your prayer shall be granted the moment
     'tis said."

The peasant, no doubt, was somewhat
    afraid,
But yet his choice was speedily made.
Humbly he lifted his hat from his head,
And, lowly bending, reverently said :
"O heavenly youth, pray think me not
    bold,
But grant, that whatever I touch, become
    gold."

The beautiful stranger raised his hand,
And touched the man with his golden
    wand.
"I would thou hadst asked more pru-
    dently,
But yet thy petition is granted thee."
He disappeared as this he said,
And heavenly odours around were shed.

"Good God," cried the peasant, "how
    rich am I !"
And at once began his new powers to try.
He touched the stem of the knotted oak,
And the sheen of gold upon him broke,
And stem, and bough, and leaf, and bud
Of glittering gold before him stood.

"Oh wonder ! Oh joy ! no more labour
    for me !
Another must now the woodcutter be !

I will eat no more but the rich and rare ;
I will drink but the wine that sparkles fair.
For the last time on my coarse bread I'll
    sup,
And drink my last draught from this
    earthen cup."

His little earthen cup he drew ;—
" How heavy it is ! How it glitters too ! "
But, alas, the liquid itself is gold ;
Not a drop of water the cup doth hold.
He raises the bread to his mouth ! Ah
    woe !
It is solid gold that hurts him so.

" Alas ! Alas ! what now shall I do ?
What has my folly brought me to ?
Can gold my hunger take away ?
Can gold this parching thirst allay ?
Oh had I, instead of gold, but bread,
And water to moisten my lips ! " he said.

The peasant awoke in pain and affright ;
For this was but a dream of the night.
" Thank God," in sudden joy he said,
" That instead of gold, I've my daily
    bread !
Thank God, that a peaceful mind I hold,
Instead of that greedy desire for gold ! "

"'Tis well, as my dream hath clearly
    shown,
God grants not all our hearts would own.
For gold in abundance many would pray,
Who with it would never be cheerful and
    gay.
Man asks for much with thoughtless mind,
And seldom seeks true good to find."

THE PAINTED WINDOW.

FROM THE GERMAN OF CANON SCHMIDT.

 PILGRIM poor, of pious mind,
    Leaving his native land behind,
    With cockle shell, and staff in
  hand,
Journeyed full far from land to land.
He saw the poor oft sore oppressed,
The bad, in stars and ribands dressed.
Naught but confusion met his glance;
And all appeared the sport of chance.

His journey, one tempestuous day,
Through a rude, pathless desert lay.
The sky with clouds was overspread;
The storm beat fiercely on his head;

When lo ! a little chapel stood,
Ancient and moss-grown, in the wood.
With reverent step his way he made
Into the chapel's darksome shade.

The pointed arch, the walls around,
All bare and unadorned he found.
The little altar of grey stone
Was with green mould quite overgrown ;
Above the altar he could trace
The only window in the place ;
Its panes, with black and red besmeared,
A dark and aimless daub appeared.

" Pah ! " cried the pilgrim with amaze,
" What work is this offends my gaze ?
Some blind man, sure, with soot and blood,
Hath painted this, in fever's mood !
Daub upon daub, smear upon smear ;—
Nor meaning, aim, nor thought appear !
Alas ! it pictures but too well
The chaos, that on earth doth dwell ! "

While thus the pious pilgrim spoke,
The sun from forth the clouds outbroke
The window, kindled by its rays,
Revealed its glories to his gaze.
A gorgeous picture he doth see
Shining in wondrous brilliancy ;

And the dim chapel's darksome night
Enhanced the more its glowing light.

The burning bush, whose wreathing flame
Tracèd Jehovah's awful name ;
The prophet, bending to the ground ;
The sheep, unconscious, grazing round ;
And purple vest, and mantle blue,
Brown rock, and meadow's verdant hue,
All, blending in one lovely light,
Beamed down upon his wondering sight.

" Ah ! " cried the pilgrim, " what a scene !
How fiery, and yet how serene !
What erst was dark, confused and drear,
Is now so sweet, so bright, so clear !
What seemed without design or thought,
Is now with deepest meaning fraught ;
And every touch, and every hue,
Reveals fresh beauty to the view."

Light o'er his darkened spirit broke,
Deep in his soul a soft voice spoke :—
" Lo ! such as this is human life !
All seems confusion, all seems strife ;
But, when the sun of Truth shines bright,
What erst was dark, becometh light.
Then trust and pray ; whate'er befall,
He ruleth well, Who ruleth all."

THE PURPLE CLOAK.

A Legend of St. Martin.

FROM THE GERMAN OF CANON SCHMIDT.

YOUTHFUL knight of noble
race
　　Rode on his steed at rapid pace;
Upon a warlike message sent,
His thoughts were on his errand bent;
Both hill and dale with snow were white,
The frost had bound each torrent tight;
Each footfall on the frozen ground
Was echoed by the hills around.

The snow was falling thick and fast;
Across the plain wild swept the blast;
It shook the warrior's feathery crest,
Nor let his golden locks have rest.
His helm and shield with ice were bound—
So keen the tempest raged around,
His purple cloak of many a fold
Could not keep out the piercing cold.

And look! an old man, poor and lame,
Whose rags scarce hide his shivering frame,
Sits trembling on the frozen ground,
While cold the snow-drifts whirl around;
And holds, the warrior's gaze to win,
His naked arms, so long and thin,—
Ah God, who hear'st each mourner's cry,
Have pity on his misery!

The knight held in his furious steed,
For sore he felt the beggar's need.
Quickly his keen-edged blade he drew,
And cut his purple cloak in two ;
And then, while tears of pity start,—
For tender was the soldier's heart,—
One half unto the beggar cast
To shield him from the biting blast.

" There, aged father," saith the knight,
" Draw that around thee warm and tight ;
And, held my scanty purse but gold,
That also would I not withhold.
Trust thou in God, for surely He
Will help thee in thy misery.
Farewell !   I dare no longer stay ;
My errand brooketh not delay."

Away he sped upon the road ;
His breast the while with gladness glowed.
O'er hill and dale he made his way
Wearing but half his mantle gay,
Until, nigh frozen with the blast,
He reached his journey's end at last;
Where many a merry jest was made,
When he his scanty cloak displayed.

But little recked the pious knight
How laughed they at his curious plight.
E'en now the midnight hour was past,
And he would fain repose at last ;

But scarce had slumber closed his eyes,
When lo ! he saw a vision rise,
Whose heavenly sweetness filled his breast
Till life in immortality had rest.

Enshrined in beams of radiant light,
Begirt with choirs of angels bright,
Whose faces bent before His throne,
While golden clouds around were strown,
Beyond conception sweet and fair
He saw his Lord and Saviour there,
Unfolding to his wondering sight
The Deity in truth and might.

And lo ! a cloak of purple hue
The Saviour round His shoulders drew,
Which, falling on the warrior's eyes,
His bosom filled with glad surprise.
His eager and astonished gaze
Beheld with wonder and amaze
The mantle he, that very day,
Threw to the beggar on his way.

Then, pointing to the purple cloak,
The Saviour to the angels spoke :
" Behold the generous gift," said He,
" Martin to-day hath given to Me !
For what upon the poor is spent,
Is only to the Saviour lent ;
And when shall come the Judgment Day,
The gift I will with interest pay."

THE CROSSES.

FROM THE GERMAN OF CHAMISSO.

 PILGRIM, who had scaled the mountain height,
Beheld beyond the valleys widely spread,
And clothèd all in evening's chasten'd light.

Upon the odorous grass he made his bed ;
(The setting sun still shed its beams around),
And, ere he slept, his vesper prayer he said.

His weary eyes were soon in slumber bound ;
But from the covering of this earthly clod
A vision raised his spirit from the ground

The sun appeared the countenance of God,—
The firmament, His gorgeous robe of state,—
And on the earth in majesty He trod.

" Wilt thou, O Lord, Who all things didst create,

Turn from me Thy dear countenance in
    scorn,
Who here confess to Thee my hapless
    state ?

Full well I know that man, of woman born,
Must bear his cross while he on earth doth
    stay ;
Yet is by each a different burthen borne.

And mine,—it is too great. I humbly
    pray
Thou'lt grant a cross that fits my feeble-
    ness,
And kindly take this grievous one away."

Childlike did he this humble prayer
    address,—
When lo ! there came a mighty wind, that
    bore
The suppliant upward with resistless stress.

And, when he stood on solid ground once
    more,
He was within a roomy hall, alone,
And saw around him crosses in great store.

Then spake a voice to him with solemn
    tone :

" Behold all ills that human life molest ;
Choose thou the burthen thou wouldst
    call thine own."

From cross to cross the pilgrim makes his
    quest,
Seeking to find, from all he seeth there,
The one that fits his bending back the best.

This is too large, and that he cannot bear ;
And, tho' a third is small and passing light,
Its edges keen his tender shoulders tear.

He seeth one—as gold it shineth bright—
He cannot pass it by untried ; but lo !
Its golden glitter gilds a golden weight !

And now he raiseth this, now that. But
    no,
The pilgrim's choice no single burthen
    won,
No cross with ease would on his shoulders
    go.

At length he hath assayed them every one ;
Lost toil ! he hath assayed them all in vain ;
The weary task must once again be done.

But, as he turned to make the search again,

H

He saw a simple cross, unseen before ;
And to examine this was now full fain.

Though from the tree of pain, the pilgrim
    bore
This cross with ease. Upon his knees he
    fell,
And said : " Lord, this I bear till life is
    o'er."

But as he gazed upon the cross, the spell
Fell off, that darken'd his dull eyes
    before ;—
It was the very cross he knew so well ;—
He raised it up, and never murmured more.

———

ABDALLAH.

FROM THE GERMAN OF CHAMISSO.

ABDALLAH rests in quiet
    by the desert fountain's side,—
    His fourscore camels round him,
the wealthy merchant's pride.
To Bassorah he had taken
    his goods,—a costly store,—
And with unladen camels
    now seeks Bagdad once more.

And lo ! a holy dervish
  draws nigh with staff in hand ;
From Bagdad he hath travelled
  on foot across the sand.
Then greet they each the other,
  and sit together there,
And drink from out the fountain,
  and praise its waters rare.

And soon hath each the other
  asked what he fain would learn ;
And each the other's questions
  hath answered in his turn.
Of this thing and of that
  they have together spoken,
And then a silence follows,
  a silence long unbroken.

But to the merchant turning
  the dervish spoke at last :
" Near to this very fountain
  I know a treasure vast.
One could from out that treasure,
  so countless is the store,
Load all your eighty camels,
  and then a thousand more."

Abdallah stares astonished ;—
  he sees the gleaming gold ;—

Cold runs his blood ;—the glamour
    his very soul doth hold.
" My brother, oh, my brother,"
    he to the dervish cried,
" Lead thou me quickly thither
    this very eventide.

" Come, and my fourscore camels
    with treasure we will load ;—
My camels are but eighty ;—
    come, thou shalt show the road.
And then, oh, then, my brother,
    thy service to repay,
The best of all my camels
    is thine this very day ! "

Then spake the dervish : " Brother,
    Such bargain may not be;
Take forty of the camels,
    and forty give to me.
The worth of forty camels
    thou'lt have a million-fold ;—
And think, had I ne'er spoken
    of this treasure and this gold ! "

" Agreed, agreed, my brother ! "
    Abdallah straight did say ;
" We will share alike the treasure,
    but let us haste away ! "

He spake, but spake with sorrow ;
    for like a millstone press'd
The thought of his forty camels
    upon the merchant's breast.

Abdallah and the dervish
    arose without delay ;
The merchant led the camels,
    the dervish showed the way.
And soon they reached a mountain,
    where an opening, strait and small,
Led to a narrow valley,
    like a doorway through a wall.

Cliffs steep and overhanging
    closed in the vale all round ;
Seldom that lonely valley
    the foot of man had found.
They halt ; and while Abdallah
    the camels doth divide,
The dervish straight advances
    unto the mountain's side.

A pile of withered brushwood
    and herbage soon he raised ;
And soon the sparks flew upward,
    and soon the bonfire blazed.
Then while the flames ascending
    filled cliff and vale with light,
With words and signs mysterious
    he cast in drugs of might.

'The black smoke quickly covered
    all in its murky fold ;
The earth, it shook beneath them ;
    above the thunder rolled ;
But, when the smoke had scattered,
    and brightly shone the day,
Lo ! in the side of the mountain
    a door wide open lay.

They entered ; and around them
    on gorgeous halls they gazed
Of precious stones and metals
    by mighty genii raised.
High rose on golden pillars
    a crystal roof o'erhead,
Whence glittering carbuncles
    a glorious daylight shed.

And between the golden pillars
    in countless store there lay
The precious gold, whose glitter
    men's reason takes away ;
And, with the gold commingling
    in heaps upon the ground
The diamond and ruby
    and emerald were found.

Abdallah stares astonished ;—
    he sees the gleaming gold ;—
Cold runs his blood ;—the glamour
    his very soul doth hold.

They set to work; the dervish
   stores up each precious stone,
But the merchant loads his camels
   with the glittering gold alone.

Yet soon he sees his error,
   and casts the gold away,
And the diamond and ruby
   upon his beasts doth lay;
But the riches he doth gather
   delight not so his mind,
As grieveth him the treasure
   that perforce he leaves behind.

The camels soon are laden,—
   laden beyond their strength,
And Abdallah to his sorrow
   must cease his task at length;
When lo! he sees the dervish,
   from an opening in the wall
At the end of a distant passage,
   take a casket mean and small.

Of common wood 'twas fashioned;
   and, as the merchant deemed,
Held naught but simple ointment,—
   all valueless it seemed;
But the holy dervish scanned it
   with keen and eager eye,
And then within his bosom
   concealed it carefully.

Now stepped they forth together,
   and stood upon the plain,
And, as the cave had opened,
   so did it close again ;
The mountains closed together,
   while earth with thunder shook,
And the merchant and the dervish
   each his share of treasure took.

Back to the desert fountain
   their journey now they make,
For there the paths divided,
   which each of them should take ;
Then give they to each other
   of peace the parting kiss,
And the dervish turns to that side,
   the merchant turns to this.

But as Abdallah turnèd,
   his heart with envy toss'd,
And the treasure of the dervish
   he deemed that he had lost.
" A dervish with such riches !
   my forty camels too !
What can a holy dervish
   with such a treasure do ? "

He turned and cried : " My brother,
   now hearken unto me !

I think not of my profit,
   I only think of thee!
Thou knowest not what sorrow,
   thou knowest not what care,
With thy treasure and thy camels
   for thyself thou dost prepare.

"Thou knowest not how vexing
   these animals can be;
Believe me, who have known them
   from earliest infancy.
With forty beasts to govern,
   I pity thee thy lot!
Thirty thou mightest manage
   —but forty thou canst not."

Then quickly to Abdallah
   the dervish thus replies:
"What thou hast said, my brother,
   I think is very wise.
Take of my forty camels
   ten most unto thy mind;
I would not that my brother
   should deem I am unkind."

Abdallah took and thanked him,
   and turned once more away.
"If I had ask'd for twenty,
   the fool had not said nay!"

He said ; and, turning backward,
   the dervish call'd again ;
Who stood, and waited for him
   upon the desert plain.

" My brother, oh, my brother,"—
   'twas thus Abdallah cried—
" Thou canst not thirty camels
   across this desert guide !
Thou knowest not how vexing
   these animals can be !
Thou surely wouldst do wisely
   to give ten more to me ! "

Then quickly to the merchant
   the dervish thus replies :
" What thou hast said, my brother
   I think is very wise.
Take of my thirty camels
   ten most unto thy mind ;
I would not that my brother
   should deem I am unkind."

But, when what scarce he hoped for
   was gainèd with such speed,
The bosom of Abdallah
   was filled with greater greed.
Without delay or scruple
   for more he askèd then ;—
First ten of the last twenty,
   then nine of the last ten.

And now the merchant's bosom
    with greed so fierce doth swell
He hasteneth to ask for
    the last of all as well.
" The camel and its burthen,
    what are they unto thee ?
Thou surely wouldst do wisely
    to give them unto me ! "

" Take the camel and its burthen,
    if so it please thy mind ;
I would not that my brother
    should deem I am unkind.
Thou hast now such a treasure,
    as man ne'er had before ;—
Depart in peace, and wisely
    employ thy priceless store."

Abdallah took and thanked him,
    but in his mind he thought :
" The dervish seems to value
    these riches as if naught !
'Tis sure the box of ointment
    he beareth in his breast !
How carefully he scanned it,
    ere he hid it in his vest ! "

And again unto the dervish
    the envious merchant spake :

"The little box of ointment,
   say, wherefore didst thou take?
What pleasure can a dervish
   in such poor trumpery find?"
"Take it," replied the dervish,
   "if so it please thy mind!"

And now a pleasing terror
   the merchant's soul possess'd,
For the casket so mysterious
   within his hand doth rest.
He thanks the holy dervish,
   then asketh him again:
"What wondrous virtue is it
   this ointment doth contain?"

The dervish said: "This ointment,
   if smeared on thy left eye,
Will all the wealth discover,
   that hid in earth doth lie;
But the right if thou besmearest,
   so wondrous is its might,
Never again with either
   shalt thou behold the light."

And now Abdallah burnèd
   to test without delay
Upon himself the virtues
   that in the ointment lay.

" Fain would I, oh, my brother,
    earth's many treasures see,—
My left eye now, I pray thee,
    quickly anoint for me."

'Tis done, and underneath him
    he turns his wondering eye ;
And lo ! in veins and caverns
    the yellow gold doth lie ;
The diamond, the ruby,
    metal and precious stone,
With fascinating glitter
    on every side they shone.

Abdallah stares astonished,
    he sees the glittering gold,
Cold runs his blood, the glamour
    his very soul doth hold.
He thinks : " And if this ointment
    besmeared the other eye,
Perchance then all these treasures
    within my reach would lie."

" My brother, oh my brother,
    hear me, I pray, once more !
Anoint my right eye also,
    as the left thou didst before.
To grant me this one favour,
    I pray thee, be not loth,—

Then part we from each other,
  and Allah bless us both ! "

Then said the holy dervish :
  " I truthfully have told
The virtues that this ointment
  doth in itself enfold ;
And wilt thou that the giver
  of wealth so vast and rare
Shall be the being hapless,
  who drives thee to despair ? "

But now the merchant's bosom
  with envy glowed the more,
And he thought : " This holy dervish
  for himself would keep the store ! "
He felt this one denial
  as fuel to his fire,
And now he urged with anger
  his covetous desire.

He said : " What to the one eye
  hath given a greater light,
Cannot, upon the other,
  deprive them both of sight.
Anoint the right eye also,
  as the left thou didst before,
Then go upon thy journey,
  for I shall ask no more."

The merchant now prepared him
   by force to gain his will,
And the holy man consented
   his wishes to fulfil.
As the left he hath anointed,
   anoints he now the right ;
And lo ! Abdallah's vision
   is quenched in endless night !

" Oh, dervish, crafty dervish,
   thou saidst the truth," he cries ;
" Now heal, I pray, the mischief ;
   restore to me mine eyes."
But the holy dervish answered :
   " Thou hast what thou hast sought ;
Go, suffer now with patience
   the sorrow thou hast wrought."

Upon the sand he wallowed ;
   he prayed, he cried, in vain ;
The dervish turnèd from him,
   and heeded not his pain ;
He took the fourscore camels,
   and went upon his way,
And by the desert fountain
   the wretched merchant lay.

Night came, and morning followed ;
   he lay in death-like swoon,

Nor felt the chill of evening,
   nor burning heat of noon ;
Three days had passed ; a pilgrim
   the desert fountain sought,
And with him unto Bagdad
   the sightless beggar brought.

———

THE SONG OF THE SWORD.

FROM THE GERMAN OF KŒRNER.

MY sword, what may I deem
   Doth mean that gladsome gleam ?
   So fond thou smil'st on me,
My heart beats joyously !
               Hurrah !

" A valiant knight art thou,—
Hence I with gladness glow !
The weapon of the free
The sword hath joy to be.
               Hurrah ! "

Free am I, trusty sword ;
And for that noble word
I love thee like a bride,
Brave weapon by my side,—
               Hurrah !

" My life I give to thee.
Thy bride I long to be.
Oh ! for the happy tide !
When takest thou thy bride ?
                    Hurrah ! "

The trumpet's voice shall say
When comes the bridal day,
When loud the cannons roar,
I wed thee,—not before.
                    Hurrah !

" Would that the day were mine !
With eagerness fierce I pine.
Bridegroom, hasten for me,—
My bridal-wreath's for thee.
                    Hurrah ! "

Within thy sheath I feel
Thee clang, my noble steel.
What is it stirreth thee ?
Thou clang'st impatiently.
                    Hurrah !

" Oh for the battle day !
Oh for the fierce affray !
A soldier's bride to be
I clang impatiently.
                    Hurrah ! "

                    I

Be still, brave sword, be still !
Beloved, what is thy will ?
Within thy sheath abide,—
Soon comes our marriage-tide.
                    Hurrah

" Oh how I long to come
Unto my garden home,
With roses bloody red
And with the scattered dead !
                    Hurrah ! "

Come forth unto the sky,
Thou apple of mine eye !
Forth from thy chamber come,
Unto my father's home !
                    Hurrah!

'Tis glorious to be here,
With such wild wedding cheer !
How in the sun's red beams
The beauteous bride-steel gleams !
                    Hurrah !

Rise, noble Teutons, rise !
Rise, hardy warriors, rise !
Do not your bosoms glow ?
Your sword-brides spurn not now !
                    Hurrah !

Before, your left upon,
With stolen glance she shone ;
Now at your right, a bride,
In God she doth confide.
                    Hurrah !

Press now the glowing steel
Upon your lips, and feel
Her kisses burning tide.
Curse him who leaves his bride !
                    Hurrah !

Sing, my beloved, sing ;
Spring, glowing fire-sparks, spring !
Now 'tis our marriage tide !
Hurrah ! my iron bride,
                    Hurrah !

THE END.

S. Cowan & Co., Printers, Perth.

www.ingramcontent.com/pod-product-compliance
Lightning Source LLC
Chambersburg PA
CBHW020406030726
47496CB00007B/2322